Dear Mom and Dad,
It's terrific here! I like ALL the girls in my bunk
and I love swimming and arts and crafts. There's
only one thing I don't like—cleaning up. And we
have to do it every single day. Why? I'll tell you.

3

We have eight people in this one little cabin. No, wait, make that ten. Our two counselors, Kit and Jackie, sleep here too.

So it gets messy pretty fast with all those people around. I don't mind the mess, and most of the girls feel the same way.

But the counselors say they have a great
idea to make cleaning up fun. That's okay with me.
I like fun!

Lots of love,

Annie

P.S. Would you please send my Godzilla mask?

Dear Mom and Dad,

Well, the fun turned out to be teams.

Kit and Jackie divided the eight of us into halves. So we were two equal teams. Four girls on each team.

Then Kit divided the bunk in half by
drawing an imaginary line right through the
middle.

My friend Judy and I made a real line out of
socks, but the counselors said it was messy.
The socks got all dirty, so we had to wash
them and put them away—neatly!
    Grumble. Groan.

Anyway, the counselors had one team clean half the bunk each morning while the other team cleaned the other half. That wasn't what I call fun.

After clean-up, we go swimming.

Half the kids are Angelfish and half are Goldfish.

I'm an Angelfish. We are COOL.

Love and kisses,

Annie

P.S. Send cookies.

Dear Mom and Dad,
    You won't believe what happened.
We forgot about the bathroom!

Neither team wanted to clean even half the bathroom. We had enough work already. So dividing us and the bunk in half didn't work. We needed another team.

I had a good idea. Actually, it was great.

"Let's divide into three equal teams," I said.
"Each team will be a third. One team will clean
the bathroom. One team will clean half of the
bunk. And one team will clean the other half."

Well, it WAS a great idea. But then Toby
said that you can't divide eight people into
three equal teams.

We still didn't know what to do. I said maybe we should ask our moms to come and clean up for us. Ha! Ha! Just kidding.

Toby said, "What if a counselor helps? Then we'll have nine people. It's easy to divide nine into thirds—three on a team."

Guess what? Kit and Jackie both said no.

Oh gosh, I'm late for swimming. Got to go. The Angelfish are about to become the Winnerfish!

Love,

Annie

P.S. How are my turtles? Don't forget, they like to eat worms out of your hand.

Dear Mom and Dad,

　Here's what happened next. I still liked the idea of three teams. "What if we had three teams of two girls each?" I said. "Then two girls could be leftovers."

Well, the leftovers didn't mind a bit. But guess what? It turned out no one wanted to be on a team. Everyone wanted to be a leftover.

So we decided to divide into fourths. We could have two girls on each team—four equal teams. The first team would clean half the cabin.

The second team would clean the other half.

The third team would clean the bathroom.
I was on that team. Lucky me.

The fourth team would pull weeds
near the porch.

It didn't work out. And not only that.
The Goldfish beat the Angelfish. Boo hoo.

Your sad daughter,

Annie

P.S. Please send more cookies!

Dear Mom and Dad,

Are you wondering why fourths didn't work out?

Bees!

One of the weed pullers got stung. They went on strike. We had to think again.

While we were thinking, we had a cartwheel contest.
It was neat—I did half a cartwheel!

I was upside down when all of a sudden
Judy said, "Teams, shmeams! I know what
we can do!"

Judy was all excited. "We can divide into eighths. There are eight girls in our bunk. So each girl is one - eighth of the group. We'll each be a team of one!"

What an excellent idea! That way
everyone could do the job she likes best.

Naomi loves to sweep. So she did the floors.
Toby and Jo like to scrub. They made the sink
and shower shine. Judy is a dust demon. She even
brought a feather duster to camp!

Every single person has a favorite job.

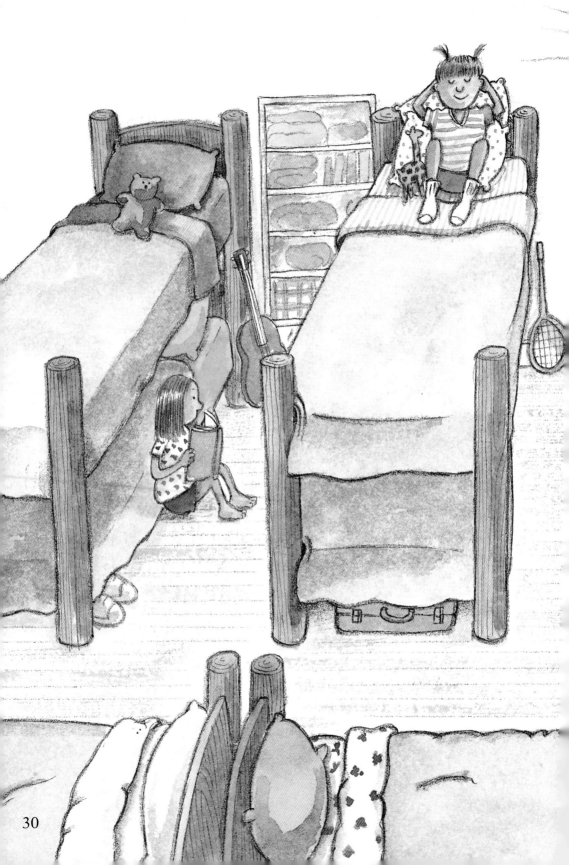

The Golden Broom Award
for Cleanest Bunk

Now I like everything about camp—
even cleaning up!

Your loving daughter,

Annie

P.S. I still won't like cleaning up at home!

FRACTION CHART

It's Sports Day! Try putting 12 campers into equal teams.

Here are some ways.

1. Halves　　　　2 equal teams

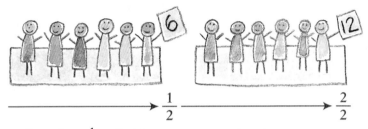

Tell why $\frac{1}{2}$ of 12 campers is 6 campers.

2. Thirds　　　　3 equal teams

Tell why $\frac{2}{3}$ of 12 campers is 8 campers.

3. Fourths　　　　4 equal teams

Tell why $\frac{3}{4}$ of 12 campers is 9 campers.